Maidoa life is never easy. They mate in pods of three, but first they must survive, then once they find each other, it's love at first sight.

Naidon and Alooma lose their meeraid—the third part of a maidoa pod. Naidon has his eye set on a new meeraid to join their fold. But Sade has other plans, and his rejection could have life or death consequences.

Collective of Love

ISBN: 978-1-4874-3239-3
Cover art by Martine Jardin

Published by eXtasy Books Inc or
Devine Destinies, an imprint of eXtasy Books Inc

Look for us online at:
www.eXtasybooks.com or www.devinedestinies.com

Collective of Love
A Maidoa Love Story 1

By

Melissa E Costa

CHAPTER ONE: NAIDON

Naidon dug his claws into the lining of his egg. Phlegm snagged between his webbed fingers and stretched over his head until he finally tore through. He opened his eyes, letting in the moisture around him. Breathing in deeply, he filled his gills with the air in the methane water. He licked the remnants of the sticky phlegm off his lips, tasting its salty flavor. It had been what nurtured him for all the months of incubation. Now he washed it down with the tasteless methane.

Naidon wiggled out from the last of the thick linings of his egg, stretching his tail and limbs.

From his parentals' memories imprinted upon him, he knew his name, and that he was part of the Maidoa race. He also knew he was of type udon, named for their black skin. Most importantly, he knew he had little time to make it to his destination.

A plethora of eggs was clustered around him. To stop the eggs from floating away, Naidon knew their udon parentals had stuck them on the bottom of the fissure. Above him, giant bubbles spewed from jets along the rocky walls. Eventually, they formed a stream that spouted from the opening at the top of the fissure. A sliver of murky light came from above. Other than the glowing red eggs, it provided the only light source.

That was where he needed to go.

Other udons ripped from their eggs. They all looked similar, like there were a million copies of himself. Some larger and fitter than others, but still having the same jet-black, circular eyes. The same small dorsal fin above the unibrow that ran along the scalp and receded down the spine.

The group of udons rushed to the opening at the top towards the light.

Naidon's muscles strained to move in the heavy liquid methane, but he forced his body onward, using his webbed hands, strong arms, and long brawny tail to propel through the dense liquid. Once outside the fissure, it would be easier to swim in the open ocean. He just had to make it there.

The lead swimmers were fast, but Naidon kept up, passing some of the smaller udons that struggled in the crushing weight. His perfect physique resulted from hundreds of years of parental improvements to his DNA and made him resilient to the crushing gravity.

He didn't want to be left behind. Feeders on the hunt for stragglers patrolled the opening. He knew a great deal about the feeders from his parental memories—specifically, his udon parental's contributions from whom he was cloned.

An udon in front of him floundered. Unlike Naidon, this one had a stumpy tail. A defect? Those happened.

After getting the other's attention, Naidon tried to grab his hand. "Here, let me help—"

"Huh?" The udon pulled free. "What are you doing? You're an udon."

"And you're in trouble! Do you want to make it to your pod or not?"

The udon seemed to weigh his options. A group of udons raced by in a frenzy, knocking him out of their way.

To increase their chances of survival, they needed to reach the currents created by the fissure's jets. This would provide them the necessary speed to not get caught by the feeders once they were out in the open.

"Well, come on, it's now or never!" Naidon said.

The stumpy-tailed udon hesitated. "W-Why should I trust

you? You might want to devour me."

An udon could absorb another udon. Naidon was only a few minutes into his life, but instinctually, he knew how—not like he ever would. His parental memories, probably incorporated from another culture they harvested, taught him to rise above that behavior.

"I won't," Naidon promised. "But the feeders will."

Finally, the udon relaxed. "Okay. Let's go."

The moment he consented, Naidon linked their hands, feeling the suction cups on their webbed fingers stick to each other. It felt too intimate. Too naked. Too personal. Immediately, he released the other udon.

"What's wrong?" The udon's eyes widened in shock.

"Just hang onto my tail." Naidon used his powerful upper body to swim through the methane, so a little extra strain on his tail from a passenger wouldn't slow him down much.

They passed one of the jets spewing from the cave wall. It was best to avoid the spout—otherwise, they might get killed from the force—and enter up ahead, when the current, while swift, wouldn't be overwhelming.

"Thanks," the other udon said.

A few more swims up, and they entered the current. Immediately, it jettisoned them out of the fissure and into the open waters. Not a second too late.

Feeders rushed in front of the mouth of the cave.

Three other udons were too slow. A rope net dragged by an approaching feeder snagged two of them, and large reptilian jaws from another feeder caught the last one. As it munched on its meal, the udon's purplish blood colored the water.

Naidon fought the urge to go back and save them. He didn't have time. Already he could feel his bolooa and meeraid—the last two types of maidoa that made up his pod. His meeraid's signature was growing weaker. Naidon had to be quick.

It was harder for sunlight to reach the bottom of the ocean, so the waters around them were murky, and if not for Naidon's evolved eyesight, he would be lost. But as the current carried him upward, it became a deep blue.

Staying inside the stream provided him extra speed, and as he didn't have the stumpy tail like the udon he'd saved, Naidon whizzed by the others.

A rather large udon swam up ahead. He was bigger than Naidon, but not by much.

"Hang on!" Naidon swished his powerful tail to pick up speed, his dorsal fin making him glide through the watery substance.

The stumpy-tailed udon dug his claws into Naidon's skin, probably so he wouldn't fall off. Those, too, must have been defective, for it didn't hurt.

As Naidon passed by, the larger udon took a swipe at him and caught his tail.

Shit.

He didn't have time to fight. Naidon needed to find his pod—especially his meeraid. He was their protector. If he failed to save them, they wouldn't last long.

With a thrust of his mighty tail, Naidon dislodged the other's grip. Turning, he charged the larger udon.

They crashed into each other. The force knocked them out of the current and into the calm but heavy murky waters. Naidon extended his fangs and bit the bigger udon's face—his teeth tearing through the other's nostril slits. Purple blood seeped into the water around them.

The larger udon slashed his claws at Naidon, who caught his hand and attacked with his own claws.

The attacker shoved away, cradling his injury, but he looked ready to strike again. That was when he noticed the stumpy-tailed udon, who'd also been knocked from the current. When the little udon saw the larger one's focus on him, he floundered and tried to get back inside the stream. But in the dense methane, his stumpy tail didn't allow for fast movement.

The larger udon caught him, trapping him in his arms. The suctions on his webbed fingers stuck to the stumpy-tailed udon's skinny body.

"Help!" he cried to Naidon, but the larger udon had already started to consume him.

Naidon charged the enemy—he couldn't watch someone die again.

The udon dodged into the current, using it to avoid Naidon's attack. "Shouldn't you be going along? Your bolooa and meeraid are waiting." He increased in size as he consumed the stumpy udon.

A stabbing pain jeered through Naidon's consciousness. *His meeraid!* Something had happened to him.

"Sorry," Naidon said to the little udon, and he meant it.

"No, wait!" the stumpy-tailed udon cried before soft yelps tore from his throat as the larger udon consumed him with full force. It was too late to help him now.

Naidon dashed into the stream. He couldn't come back. The larger udon would be even bigger. Of course, stumpy hadn't been much of a meal, but even so, that would still make the other udon more of a challenge. Naidon didn't fear losing, as his udon parental had honed their skills. He could probably still win against the larger udon and maybe even consume him as well, but there wasn't time.

Another painful spike made his head dizzy. His meeraid was in trouble.

The higher he ascended, the easier it became to swim, but his weight and size made him slower. Thankfully, his aerodynamic body counteracted this disadvantage, and he shot through the liquid methane, his dorsal fin cutting through the water.

It was substantially brighter up there as well, the methane shimmering a brilliant blue. But Naidon had no time to admire the scenery. He was close to his meeraid. He could feel it. He had to make it, had to save him. Failure was not an option.

Chapter Two: Sade

Sade breathed in his first waking breath, finally ready to come out of incubation. Inside his mind, flashes of parental memories told him about himself and his environment. He was a juvenile maidoa of the meeraid type. They were named for their red skin and made up the third part of a maidoa pod. Sade's podmates awaited him, much in the same way his parentals and their parentals before them had done. Technically, he was an offspring of all three of his parentals' types—meeraid, bolooa, and udon, but for all practical purposes, he was a clone of his meeraid parental.

He opened his eyes, blinking. Beyond the film that covered him, everything looked opaque, but movement came from all around him. His incubation bed was encased in the wall behind him. He twitched his webbed fingers, using his claws to tear open the film keeping him attached. When he freed his hands, it was easier to work on the rest of his body. The point of his long, skinny tail got caught in the film's gummy texture, and he needed to give it an extra tug.

Now free from the wall, he found himself in a very cramped cave. All around him, other meeraids were in various phases, from some still stuck in the wall, eyes still shut, to others almost out—with only hands or tails still attached.

Light showed from what looked like the cave's opening. The meeraids swam for the exit, Sade along with them. It appeared they'd been in a fissure in a large cliff that rose so high he couldn't see the top. The water above shimmered from the sunlight.

The other meeraids blindly ascended the wall, their tails wiggling back and forth as they swam, following their instincts to their bolooas waiting for them at the top.

Sade sensed his own bolooa calling to him.

He scoffed, his tiny nostril slits flaring. She didn't want *him* specifically. He was just the designated meeraid in her pod. This was all predestined.

Sade didn't want to join some colossal glob, which was what would happen if he swam to his bolooa. Together the two would wait for their udon and then they would become one—a complete maidoa adult.

Sade shook his head. *No, thank you!*

Whereas the group swam up, Sade swam down. The pull toward his pod only grew stronger, but he ignored it. He was going to be himself, not another clone.

The farther he swam down, the more meeraids he saw. Some hadn't been incubating inside one of the fissures but on the wall directly. Their parentals must have come to the Birthing Wall late in the game, and they weren't able to get a good spot inside.

They pulled themselves free and started swimming for the top towards the Pearl Petals where the bolooas were located.

Sade ignored them and kept going. As he swam, his lithe and slender body wiggled along with his tail. The flow of water felt amazing over his soft and bendy fin that went from the crown of his head to the tip of his tail. He was alive. He was free.

A larger, rather attractive meeraid crossed his path. "You're going the wrong way."

He shrugged. "What's it to you?"

The other meeraid raised his unibrow. "Fine, go. But only feeders await meeraids like you who don't swim upward."

Like Sade cared. He swam faster, then paused. Why did he need to hug the wall at all? He had the whole ocean.

He gazed out at the nothingness beyond the Birthing Wall—only ocean, deep and cool. He swam out into the open waters. With every bit of distance he put between himself and his bolooa, the less he ached inside. Like he was being freed from them.

A dark shadow came from above, rapidly nearing the Birthing Wall.

Feeders!

There were so many that they blocked the light like a single mass.

Meeraids tried to escape, but the feeders intercepted them one by one. They torpedoed into the fleeing crowd. Their jaws opened, their thick reptilian tails stirring up bubbles in the water, filled with the blood of their prey.

Screams. Cries.

The jaws of a large feeder snatched up the meeraid he'd spoken to only moments ago. Some feeders dragged nets to catch the juveniles. But this one, like so many others, must have been hungry.

He chomped down on the meeraid's midsection, and more purple blood colored the water.

A battle cry sounded, and a dark figure charged into the feeder.

It was an udon. What was he doing here? Udons started out in caves deep on the ocean's floor and in the opposite direction of the Birthing Wall. Meeraids and udons were only supposed to meet on the pearl petals when they came to their bolooa.

The udon succeeded in knocking the feeder off course.

Sade studied his robust and shapely body—muscular chest, chiseled abdomen, and sculped arms—with a powerful tail and stern-looking, jet-black eyes. He was quite beautiful. *Interesting*. His eyes held a challenge, a fight to them that Sade thought no one else in the world understood except himself. This maidoa wouldn't just accept his fate. He would fight.

Would he win against a feeder? Even one that large?

Sade wanted to stick around and see, but staying there would be dangerous. He needed to leave before he was spotted. Still, he didn't want to go without knowing the outcome. He wanted this udon to win.

The udon rushed toward the feeder, who puffed out water from its two protruding nostrils, then charged. The body of the meeraid hung from its jaws. Lifeless.

The moment before they collided, the udon darted out of the way, grabbing the meeraid. He tugged, but the feeder's jaws locked deep, and more purple blood was added to the water. The udon cried in agony. He swam past the feeder and out into open water before he circled back.

The feeder munched hungrily, swallowing down the meeraid's remains.

The look of anguish and hatred in the udon's black, circular eyes pierced Sade's soul. Perhaps that meeraid belonged to the udon's pod? Sade's heart ached for them both.

Claw-tipped hands snatched Sade from behind. *A feeder!* Unlike the one who had devoured that meeraid, this one threw him into a large net.

The udon's gaze found his. It was only for a moment, but a feeling of familiarity washed over Sade. He didn't know this udon, nor was he part of Sade's original pod. Still, there was something in those jet-black eyes. Desperation? Despair? Interest, maybe? Whatever it was, Sade couldn't see for long. The feeder dragged him deeper and deeper until he could no longer see the udon still fighting.

Chapter Three: Alooma

Alooma opened her eyes. She lay on a soft petal that swayed in the current—her tentacles that made up her lower body savored its silky smoothness.

Blue waters of liquid methane shimmered above. From this distance, she could see the topmost surface of the last oceanic layer, looking like a line of glistening silver.

As she inhaled, her breasts rose with each breath. The gills on her neck fluttered, drawing in nitrogen from the planet's ocean and letting it fill her lungs.

"I'm alive," she whispered. Her mesoglea skin tingled in the gentle water. Long plumes flowed from her head and around her waist. She traced her fingers down her face, feeling the smooth curve from her crescent eyes to the slits of her nostrils, and finally to her full lips.

She looked around. Small patches of white sand peeked through the oversized mother-of-pearl petals from the plants that grew on top of the sand dunes. Unlike the other two members of her pod, bolooas were not born in clusters. She could barely see the other bolooas some distance away—all of them, like her, were waking up.

Instinct flooded Alooma, drawing her attention to her pod. "Where's my udon and meeraid?" The moment she thought about her meeraid her stomach burned with a sheering pain, and she screamed.

"No . . . no!" She wanted to rush to her dying mate. The Birthing Wall scaled the plateau where the Pearl Petal plants grew, but she didn't have a clear line of sight—not without leaving her current spot. If she did that, how would her udon find her? If anyone could protect her and their meeraid, it was him.

But what if it was already too late for their meeraid?

"No!" Angrily, she shook her head. "That's not true!" It was futile to yell at the watery sky as if their parentals could hear from the atmosphere bordering outer space, but she didn't care. They were up there, somewhere, and their children needed them. But visiting their offspring wasn't what maidoa did. It was only after the juveniles became adults that they finally met their parentals.

Two nearby petals rustled, pushed aside by an incoming udon. He didn't belong to her pod. Hers wasn't even near the vicinity yet.

The udon swam between the petals, and his long black tail almost ripped one.

He eyed her. He wasn't relatively big. With her tentacles and head plumes, Alooma would always appear larger than any udon. The fact that he'd made it to the Pearl Petals so quickly spoke of his fitness.

But why her? He must have felt his bolooa calling him. Why was he pursuing Alooma? It wasn't like she was another udon that he could devour.

The look in his eyes spoke his intention. He wanted to become podmates.

"Wait!" she cried out as he advanced. His tail sent ripples through the methane as he rushed toward her, and it made the petal tremble beneath her fingertips.

Alooma couldn't let him touch her. She wouldn't join with him, regardless of how fit he was. "I'm not your mate!"

Madness shone from his jet-black eyes. "That doesn't matter. She's dead."

"Dead?" Alooma said, shocked. "That's not possible."

The udon scoffed. "Tell that to the feeders. They're more

aggressive this year. They even made it to the Pearl Petals and took her right before I could reach her."

Sadness filled her heart. She understood his desperation now. He'd lost his bolooa. If he couldn't replace her, his pod wouldn't be able to join before time was up. Then he would be stuck as a juvenile and surely become food for the feeders.

"I'm sorry for your loss, but I'm not without mates." She didn't mention her meeraid. She couldn't let herself believe that he was dead. "I can't join with you."

He scoffed. "Can't? Or won't?"

"Does it matter? No means no."

"Not in this world it doesn't!" He sprang at her.

She darted, using her tentacles to propel out of the way. "Stay back! I have an udon!"

Udons were quicker, and he trapped her in his arms. Pressing his body into hers, he tried to join with her. But they were one member short. Bolooas and udons couldn't join without a meeraid—they could meld a little, but that wasn't the same as an actual join. And even with three maidoas present, joins required willing participants.

He didn't seem to realize this, perhaps driven mad by the death of his mate. He hugged her tighter, digging his claws into her back, tearing her jelly-like skin. In his haste, he wasn't trying to join properly. At this rate, he would slice her in two.

Her purple blood colored the waters as he tore her flesh. "Stop it!" She bit his ear and would've taken off the small lobe if it wasn't tucked into his head.

He growled at her, then sank his jagged teeth into her shoulder, more of her purple blood seeping out. She scratched him wherever she could reach, tearing up his shoulders.

"I'm not your mate! Nor will I ever be. Release me!"

A low growl rumbled from behind them. Her eyes widened. It was her udon! Tall, muscular, he looked more like a god than a being. She looked over her shoulder, and the moment she saw him, she remembered his name. *Naidon*.

Naidon showed his fangs. "Release her."

The other udon stopped hurting her with his claws and pressed his palms flat against her back, now properly trying to join with her. It was madness. He wasn't going to achieve what he wanted, but his mind was too far gone. The only way to escape him was for Naidon to finish him off.

Naidon was the fighter, the protector of the pod, not bolooas or meeraids. A bolooa couldn't hope to fight off an udon, but that didn't matter. At that moment, Naidon charged. The other one had to release her to prevent getting his head sliced off.

Alooma dodged out of the way. Naidon didn't even have to tell her to move, nor did he tell her where to go to get out of his way. She simply did it—their bodies operating as if extensions of each other, falling back on instincts that were as old as the Maidoa race.

The two udons fought with fangs drawn and claws out, hitting each other with their tails.

The attacker clasped Naidon's forearms, his suctions out. He was trying to devour Naidon!

Naidon headbanged him, and the sharp edge of his fin splintered the other's skin. The udon promptly let him go and cradled his wound, looking dizzy from the impact.

Naidon clutched the other udon's back, his suctions tugging at the other's flesh as he started to absorb him. It would make Naidon stronger, but not without consequences that would mar his personality, maybe even make him cruel and unfeeling.

He was winning, absorbing his rival, who struggled in his arms.

"Don't devour him!" Alooma screamed to her mate. "Release him if you can."

At her voice, Naidon weakened his hold, and the other

udon got free and hurried off.

Bloodlust filled Naidon's jet-black eyes—beautiful in the shimmering watery world. Then his gaze found hers, and he rushed to her side. "Are you okay?" He examined her wounds with hands that only moments before had almost drained the life from another udon.

She smiled softly. "You found me."

"And just in time, too." He hugged her. "Forgive me for taking so long, Alooma." Pulling back, he rested his forehead against hers and brought their palms together. At the touch, a soothing sensation filled her, and she shut her eyes. Their fingers intertwining, their skin merged until they had nothing between them.

This was joining.

He rubbed his cheek against hers. Unlike her jelly-like skin, his was firm and coarse, but it softened as she rubbed against his.

Her hair plumes circled them, covering his body, and the pores on their skin began to connect, his rough skin becoming as jellylike as her own.

Tilting his face, he fitted their mouths together.

But they couldn't fully join. Not without their meeraid.

She yanked away. "Where's Laraid?"

Sadness shone in his eyes. And something else. *Shame.*

"I couldn't get to him in time to save him."

She backed away, shaking her head. "No . . . no!" She glanced in the direction she'd felt Laraid's presence. "No, it's not true!" A madness grew inside her, and she knew the other udon's pain.

Naidon couldn't meet her eyes. "Yes, it is. I'm so sorry."

Alooma refused to accept this outcome. Without another word, she dashed off, ducking underneath the petals. Her tentacles propelled her through the water. The petals above formed a dense canopy, but thanks to the sunlight spilling through the openings between the plants, she still could see. She swam over the white sands that covered the plateau and dazzled in the light, also helping with illumination.

Up ahead loomed a deep precipice—the Birthing Wall. It went straight down to the ocean's floor. Here along this cliff was where she would find her mate.

Chapter Four: Naidon

Naidon rushed after Alooma. Inside, his heart also ached for their meeraid. He'd been too late to save Laraid. Still, they had to go on. Their instincts demanded nothing less. And yet, Alooma seemed to have thrown all of that aside.

Naidon needed to catch up if he wanted to protect her. However, given the fury in her crescent amber eyes, he felt sure even the feeders would quiver.

They swam in the direction Naidon had taken to get to Alooma after failing to save Laraid. Finally, they reached the edge of the plateau. Bolooas weren't made for swimming in the depths, but that didn't stop Alooma. Already she had plunged into the open waters, following along the Birthing Wall.

The deeper they dove, the easier it became to keep up with Alooma as the liquid mercury became heavier, and unlike her, Naidon was made for swimming in that kind of pressure, and he caught up with her quickly.

They swam down the empty wall into an eerie silence. Only a few meeraids still lingered. Most would be gone. It was much too late in the game. Perhaps these were lost, or maybe they no longer had their pods.

Maybe going there had been a bad idea, but if they didn't find a meeraid, they wouldn't be able to become a pod. And what better place to find one than at the Birthing Wall?

Thinking of mating with another meeraid hurt more than he could bear. He wanted Laraid, but that damn feeder had killed him. Alooma looked around with wide, desperate eyes.

Her pants sent tiny bubbles out into the water.

"What now, Naidon?" Her body shook with visible tension. "Where is he? We have to find him!"

Naidon grabbed her hand and spun her to face him. "Laraid's not here. A feeder got him."

"No . . ." Large tears welled up in her eyes before the water took them away.

"I saw it . . ." Naidon hung his head. "A feeder ate—"

"The feeders!" Alooma's eyes hardened, her jaw set. She growled low in her throat. "Then that's where we're going. To the feeders."

"Alooma?"

"I'm not leaving my mate!"

Naidon searched her eyes. They couldn't afford to not find a meeraid, and going to the feeders would only cost them time and possibly their lives.

An image of another meeraid surfaced in his mind. Naidon had been fixated on trying to rescue Laraid, so at first, he hadn't noticed the other meeraid.

He must've been watching Naidon fight the feeder, but it wasn't until the feeders snagged him in a net that Naidon finally saw him. There was something about him. Naidon hadn't thought too much on it, mostly because of Alooma's call. He'd gone after Alooma, but somewhere in his heart, he never let that meeraid go.

"All right." It was for that meeraid that Naidon went to the feeder village. His *new* meeraid.

They descended into the depths, using the wall to keep track of their location. The liquid methane grew murkier and heavier, making it harder to swim. Naidon took Alooma's hand. He could see much better in this environment than she could.

At the bottom of the ocean, a wide valley stretched as far as the eye could see. Boulders littered the landscape here and there, some covered in barnacles large enough to hide inside.

Nearby were several geysers. Liquid spewed out of them in long tendrils that rushed towards the surface. Feeders didn't like the geysers, so they built their villages some distance away but still close enough to see the Birthing Wall—an opportune hunting spot.

Thick black kelp grew on the ocean floor. It wasn't very tall, so it looked like the ground was moving. Feeders normally swam on their bellies and could hide easily in the kelp.

Naidon put a hand on Alooma's shoulder. "Wait." She looked about to protest. "Let's avoid the kelp. Follow my lead." He guided Alooma around the geysers while staying high up enough to pass over the kelp.

Thankfully, feeders also disliked living among the kelp. He could tell they were approaching a village, because the ocean floor was clear, and somebody had pushed large boulders around to form a loose semi-circle. The feeders used the boulders for everything from shelter, altars, or to place their killed prey upon.

This feeder village was packed, as most had come home from their day's hunt.

Naidon sucked in a breath. This was going to be tricky. And time was a luxury that they didn't have.

They had to swim high up enough to avoid the kelp but low enough not to be spotted by the feeders. Never had Naidon felt so exposed. At any moment, a school of feeders might come their way.

They approached the village from the side. Naidon had the ability to see farther than Alooma, so he led. Around the feeder village were large cages made of thick rope. They were tied down to the rocks below, floating as much as the ropes allowed.

Maidoa were jammed inside. Mostly meeraids, but udons as well. Catching bolooas was harder, because feeders weren't made for swimming in the lighter water where the Petal Plants grew. Still, they'd managed to snag a couple. With so many captured, he wondered how their species even survived. The fact that they lost their meeraid was probably more common than he thought.

That was when he saw that one of the cages was empty. Naidon furrowed his unibrow and inched closer to see through the murky waters.

Feeders chased after maidoa that had been released from the nearby cage. Purple blood made the water even inkier. With how much of a mess they were making, it was surprising the feeders didn't bite one another. Strange that they would capture them, only to hunt them again, but that was the feeders.

"Come on!" Still holding Alooma's hand, Naidon made a break for a nearby rock that was part of the feeder village.

He'd have to scout for the cage that contained his new meeraid, but first, he had to make sure that he and his podmate didn't become part of that feeding frenzy.

They made it behind the boulder, both catching their breaths—panting mostly because of fear rather than physical exhaustion.

"Okay, let me check out the cages. Stay hidden."

Alooma nodded, although there was a question in her crescent eyes. But Naidon didn't have time to waste.

He poked his head out and scanned the cages from afar. There were five in total. One of them had already been opened and was providing entertainment for the feeders. The four others were still locked.

Where was his meeraid? Had he been eaten already? Naidon growled at the thought of those scaly monsters making yet another meal out of his dear ones.

Dear ones? He didn't even know this meeraid. Maybe he already had a pod, assuming they weren't here as well.

Then Naidon spotted him in a cage at the far end. He veered Alooma in that direction, still hugging close to the shadows the rocks provided. It made it harder to see in the already dimly lit ocean floor, but Naidon's eyes were adapted for this environment.

Two feeders approached.

Naidon hid behind the boulder they'd been keeping close to, pulling Alooma with him against his chest. He wrapped his arms around her—his black skin would hide them better than her golden plumes.

The feeders carried a meeraid and an udon. Both were tiny—which probably explained why the udon had also been captured. They took them over to a large rock where a group of feeders sat. Pinning them against the slab, they dove stakes through their wrists. They each took turns biting off chunks of their prey's bodies. The Maidoa race had never learned to communicate with the feeders, so he couldn't understand what they said to each other, but they looked to be making themselves merry with food and conversation.

Anger and sadness pooled in the pits of his stomach. Naidon had to turn away. Otherwise, he'd attack every single one of them. Behind him, another feeder opened the second cage. Immediately, those trapped in the cage rushed for the exit and swam wildly toward the surface. Some would make it. Most would not.

Feeders hovered nearby before they darted for the swimming prey.

Alooma looked away as one of the feeder's clamped his large jaws down on a fleeing meeraid. Naidon also couldn't watch. All he saw was the memory of his own beloved Laraid.

They needed to get to the cage containing their new meeraid before the feeders did.

He and Alooma moved as one and stuck close to the boulders. Swimming together in the shadows, they used the feeders' distraction to their advantage.

Three boulders were pressed together, and they caught a glimpse of a feeder living space. Dead kelp made bedding, and a few bits and pieces of food and some kind of rope weaving filled the space.

Finally, they rounded the bin where their desired cage was located. His new meeraid was packed in with mostly other meeraids, although a few udons and even a bolooa were present.

"Found him!" Naidon made sure the coast was clear. The feeders were either still busy with the hunt or else consuming meals elsewhere. "Okay," he whispered. "Now we need to open that cage."

As they approached, the captives cried out.

"Help!"

"Save us!"

"Keep quiet," Alooma scolded. "Else they'll hear us."

The closest meeraids nodded and shut their mouths.

"Okay, Naidon, go find a key, and I'll look for Laraid." She started to look over the meeraids.

Naidon clenched his eyes shut for a brief moment and exhaled sharply. "He's not there, Alooma. You know this. You can feel it."

Alooma shook her head. "Then we must keep searching!"

"He's gone." Naidon took her hands, linking their fingers. He rested his forehead against hers. "Dearest Alooma, you know it's true."

Large tears welled up in her eyes before the liquid methane carried them away. She shook her head.

"We're wasting time. If we want to survive, we must find another meeraid. And I've got one." He pointed to his meeraid in the crowd.

Alooma craned her neck. "Which one?"

He singled out the meeraid again. "You can feel it, too,

can't you? A connection to that meeraid."

Alooma tilted her head to the side. "That one?"

Naidon nodded. "There's something between us. I can't describe it, but it feels right."

Alooma yanked her hand away as if she'd been slapped. "Was this the reason you came with me? For him?"

Cries and screams rang out.

Naidon spun around. The feeders had opened a third cage. As soon as they were free, maidoas dashed in every direction. So many of them were being killed, but however horrible, it was buying Naidon and Alooma time.

"They've already opened three cages. They'll be here soon!" However much Naidon considered himself a survivor, he couldn't hope to fight an entire village of feeders.

"No, I won't join with some stranger." Alooma shook her head. "It's a disservice to our mate."

"Our mate is gone. If we don't find another, we won't survive, either."

"Then maybe we shouldn't." Despair filled her amber eyes. "I don't want to live without my beloved."

He understood her more than she realized. "I know. Skies, I know. I would rather lie down and die, but we can't. Our line needs to continue. We can't fight our destiny."

Alooma screwed her eyes shut. She balled her fists so tightly that she drew blood. Finally, she blew out a sigh of resignation. "I don't intend to."

"Then help me."

Alooma glanced at the cage, then at the surrounding foliage. "How?"

"There's got to be a key." He scanned the nearby rocks. Sure enough, a stone key was propped against a nearby ledge.

"There!" Naidon rushed to get it. And came face to face with a feeder.

Shit.

The feeder wasn't as large as some of the others Naidon had encountered. For a moment, it seemed as confused as he was. But only for a moment.

"Hey!" Alooma yelled, calling its attention. "Come and get me! You can get udons any day. But how many chances do you have at a bolooa?"

"Alooma, no!" Naidon was the faster swimmer—it was far more dangerous for her. His eyes widened in terror as he watched Alooma dart off, tentacles propelling her through the water. The feeder chased after her without bothering to alert the others.

She swam in the direction of the geysers.

Atta girl!

The current that spewed from their jets would help her swim quicker, despite her disadvantage.

Naidon couldn't tear his attention away from her. Not until she reached the geyser. The feeder was jaws away from her tentacles, but before it could bite, she got inside the current and the stream doubled her speed, thrusting her upward.

Naidon had to trust that she would make it to the fissure on the Birthing Wall. She had given him a chance to free their new meeraid, and he was wasting it.

He grabbed the key off the ledge. When he approached the cage, all the prisoners began reaching for him.

"Help!"

"Help us!"

"Shh," Naidon warned. "You'll get their attention." He unlocked the door. "Out, but in an orderly fashion. You mustn't alert them."

The meeraids and udons at the entrance of the cage nodded, and Naidon moved aside.

CHAPTER FIVE: SADE

Sade huddled near the back, his gaze drawn to the udon approaching their cage.

He was the same one who failed to save the other meeraid. What was he doing here? Why risk himself when his meeraid was already dead?

The udon's focus fixated on Sade.

"Shh," he told the other captives. "Otherwise, you'll draw their attention."

The cluster of meeraids fell silent and looked with fearful eyes at the feeders still busy hunting.

When the cage door opened, a smaller number of meeraids farther inside panicked. They swarmed the exit. One shoved Sade out of the way, and he smacked against the wall of the cage.

The udon raised his hands. "Keep calm. Don't rush!"

Nothing he said deterred them.

Sade tried to move, but his tail was caught in the netting. It must have happened when he was shoved. The rush of bodies had wedged his tail in even farther.

The udon waited outside. Was he waiting for Sade? That made so little sense. They weren't podmates.

When the last of the numbers had cleared, the udon held out his hand. "Come, this way!"

Sade tugged his tail, but it didn't budge. "I can't! I'm stuck."

The udon sucked in a breath and went to help him.

What's he doing? Who'd go inside a cage for a stranger?

The fleeing group had drawn way too much attention. Feeders chased after the maidoa, and most weren't focusing on the cage, probably assuming that it would be empty. And it was . . . all except for him and the udon.

"What's your name?" The udon grabbed Sade's shoulder, his other arm going around Sade's back. "I'm Naidon." Heat radiated from Naidon's firm, muscular body, and Sade leaned into the touch, a jolt of warmth running up his spine. It felt like he was coming home. Why his brain was even registering things so silly was an enigma, but he couldn't dwell on it for long. "Name? What is it?"

"Um, Sade."

Naidon tugged on him, trying again to free him. Pain shot up through his tail. "Ouch!" Sade cried, his tail throbbing. "I can't . . . just go! Otherwise, you'll be caught, too."

"Not happening." Naidon swam down and bit the ropes, his sharp and pointy fangs narrowly missing Sade's skin. But the rope, clearly made to keep maidoa in, was far too thick. Only a little bit frayed off.

Maidoa shouted from all around them as the feeders continued their hunt. One feeder crunched down on the arm of a fleeing udon. He tried to fight back, attacking the feeder's eyes, struggling in the feeder's grasp. So far, he looked to be hurting the feeder. Maybe he would win. A nearby meeraid wasn't so lucky, and the feeder who attacked him munched away at his broken body.

Naidon tore at the cage with his claws. Nothing.

Sade sighed. "It's useless. Just get out of here."

Chapter Six: Naidon

Naidon tugged futilely on Sade's tail before meeting Sade's red, elliptical eyes. "It's going to be okay," he said, his hand lingering on Sade's back.

"Okay? I'm about to get eaten."

Naidon bared his pointy fangs. "Not if I have anything to say about it." He swam out of the cage. Purple blood in the water from all the death made it difficult for him to see. No sooner had he left the cage than two feeders returned and started stuffing captured meeraids and udons back inside. He was losing his window to free Sade.

He eyed some nearby rocks on either side of the hovering cage. Using one to gain some momentum, he pushed off it and dove beneath the net. He rammed into Sade's tail, shoving it upward.

Sade yelped, but his tail came free.

The momentum shot Naidon out of the opposite side of the cage and over to the other rock. Pushing off it, he darted underneath the cage again, this time shoving as many meeraids and udons towards the exit as he could. The wave of water he stirred up propelled them forward, and they crashed into the ones the feeders were stuffing in, forcing the newcomers back out.

The feeders tried to contain their captives, but as Naidon continued, they stopped their futile efforts. Their reptilian eyes fixed on him, pupils reverting into slits. They looked to the adjacent rocks Naidon had been using for speed. One feeder swam to intercept him as Naidon glided toward a rock.

Naidon slowed his movement by dragging his claws along the ocean floor, then he pushed off in the opposite direction and back underneath the cage.

The second feeder darted over to the other side, waiting by that rock to intercept Naidon. Now both blocked him on either side.

They'd left the entry unguarded. Naidon darted toward the entrance. Sade lingered in the opening. He grabbed Sade's hand, and they took off swimming. The feeders chased after them, movements from their large scaly tails stirring up the sand from the ocean floor. But soon, they gave up and returned to the cage to prevent others from escaping.

Three more feeders who had previously been hunting turned their large, beady eyes on them.

"Swim!" Naidon drove through the water using his powerful tail. Sade lagged behind, which was strange, as meeraids were supposed to be the fastest swimmers of all maidoa. But given the slower way he wiggled his tail, Naidon guessed he was injured from the cage.

Up ahead, Naidon could just barely see Alooma. She swam in elegant loops, forcing the feeder to dart after her. His scaled tail wasn't adept at taking all the sharp turns, which gave Alooma the advantage. The feeder was fast, however. It gained on her.

She swam to the Birthing Wall. There were tiny fissures in it, and some looked to be deeper than others. Meeraids normally birthed inside those, as the feeders couldn't fit in the cramped space. Although she was larger compared to a meeraid, Alooma could still fit, unlike the feeder.

She propelled through the water, leaving a trail of bubbles. The feeder reached for her, its jaws opening. Before it could chomp down, she jettisoned into the fissure. Safe.

Naidon and Sade swam for the geyser stream that Alooma had used.

The feeders gained on them, the sparse light in the murky water reflecting off their pointy teeth. One swiped at Sade's tail—its sharp talons dug into his rubbery skin, and Sade cried out.

Naidon growled. He threw Sade in front of him, moving him as though Sade didn't have a tail of his own.

They were almost to the stream. Straight ahead, tendrils of current wove through the liquid mercury. All Naidon needed to do was get Sade inside of it. "Can you make it to the Birthing Wall? Once you're in the current, go to the closest fissure, and we'll meet inside." The moment they reached the bubbly waters, Naidon shoved Sade through. The rush of water shot him upward, quickening Sade's speed. Combined with his rapidly wiggling tail, he was making great time.

It was Naidon who was still in the crossfire.

The nearest feeder's jaws reached out just as Naidon caught the current. Its teeth connected, but the harsh stream yanked Naidon upward. The feeder couldn't hold on, and its tooth tore Naidon's skin. Purple blood colored the bubbles around him, and he tried not to focus on the jolts of pain. He swam as fast as he could, using his aerodynamic body . . . something the feeders didn't have.

The one who had bitten him entered the stream, but its bigger size prevented it from moving as fast. Sade, being the smallest, moved the quickest. The other two feeders swam upward along with the current but still outside it. They were way behind. At this rate, Naidon looked like he was in the clear.

That was when he saw a feeder approaching Sade. It was the one who'd chased Alooma and had been stalking the Birthing Wall. It must have decided Sade was an easier target. The current was taking Sade straight into its path.

Naidon had to reach him in time, but Sade was moving way too fast. "Get out of the stream!" Sade looked over, his red eyes large and terrified. "Trust me!"

Sade reached a hand outside of the current, and it was enough to slow him down.

Naidon picked up speed.

The charging feeder was going to make it to Sade first.

"Out of it completely," he yelled. The feeder that had entered the current behind Naidon was still chasing him. Despite having the added boost from the current, Naidon also wasn't that light, so he didn't move as fast. Now it was gaining on his tail.

Sade hesitated but pulled free from the current. The feeder couldn't stop, but this one wasn't too big. Upon entering the current, its more petite body shot upward, caught in its flow. It tried to break with its tail, but that only steered it onward. The time it would take for it to escape the stream would be enough for them to get away.

Sade made a break for the Birthing Wall, only to be cut off by another feeder. It was one of the two feeders chasing after Naidon that hadn't gotten into the current. How had it gotten there so fast?

There was absolutely no way Naidon was losing another meeraid. "Get back inside the current!"

Sade turned tail and made a break for the current, only to be caught. The feeder's claws snared his arm, and he cried out, blood coming from the wound.

Naidon burst out from the stream using the additional speed and charged the feeder, sending it spinning into open water. It didn't have a good grip on Sade, and now Naidon was more than a handful. But this one was larger than the one who'd been chasing Alooma, although not as big as the others. Perhaps its relatively smaller size was the reason it was able to catch up.

"There's another one coming!" Sade pointed over Naidon's shoulder. The feeder who had been chasing Naidon in the current hadn't given up—now it was gaining fast. Naidon might be able to handle the first feeder, but two against one? Not a chance.

Near the Birthing Wall, the thick smell of birthing juices still lingered in the water. They were close to a fissure. It would be a tight fit for him, but not for Sade.

"Get inside!" Naidon shoved Sade into it. He almost made it through, too, when teeth sank into his flipper and dragged him back outside. He howled in pain. Purple inky blood surrounded him.

"Over here!" Alooma's voice came from somewhere above him.

"Alooma, no!" Naidon shoved his claws deep inside the feeder's nostrils, drawing blood, making the green ink compete with the purple water. The feeder slashed its talons at Naidon's tail, and he winced in pain as it tore off lines of suctions from his skin. With all his might, he kicked the feeder. But it didn't let go.

Alooma dove straight into the feeder's skull and dislodged its jaws. Naidon got onto its back and slammed its jaws shut, trapping it in a tight hold. They struggled with the feeder, its tail flailing, its head shaking back and forth like it was trying to rip meat from a bone.

"You, there!" It was Sade's voice, calling to the approaching feeder. "I'm closer, and I'm slower. Come and get me."

Oh no . . .

Alooma gouged the feeder's beady eyes with her claws, and then she latched her fangs onto its throat. Juvenile maidoa were not made to fight feeders, but she and Naidon were doing okay anyway. Feeders' strengths lie in their massive jaws, not necessarily in their arms and claws.

Naidon looked up to see yet another feeder closing in. *Skies, how many are there?* That was when he remembered that they'd been chased by three feeders initially and had also encountered the one after Alooma. Hers had been dealt with—

they were fighting one, and Sade had taken the other who'd been following Naidon in the current. And now, it seemed like the last feeder had finally caught up. This one was the largest of them all, which was why it probably took it longer to swim to the waters above.

"Alooma, let go and get into the fissure!" Like they were one mind, she obeyed. Naidon held his ground, still struggling with the feeder, who had become even more frenzied after Alooma took out its eye.

The other feeder opened its jaws, coming in fast. Using all his strength, Naidon wrestled with the one he was fighting until its back faced the approaching threat.

The incoming feeder was too close to stop.

Naidon let go the moment the other feeder's jaws clamped down over its companion. Then he darted for the fissure, not stopping to see the outcome. Only when he made it inside did he look back. Green blood was everywhere—it hadn't turned out good for the feeder who'd just got munched on.

The two feeders attacked each other. The little one must have been pissed. The larger feeder didn't seem to want to fight. They were speaking to each other, but Naidon couldn't understand their language. He didn't have time to wait, either. He had to go and see what happened to Sade. Had he made it to the fissure or been devoured?

Naidon sensed Alooma's presence. In the time he'd been watching the feeders attack each other, she'd gone three fissures up. Why? Had she gone to save Sade?

The two feeders were still fighting amongst themselves, and that allowed for Naidon to make a break for it. Quickly, he jutted for the fissure she was in. "Where's the meeraid?" he said once inside.

"He made it into the current again." It wasn't what Naidon wanted to hear, but at least it was better than hearing that the feeder got to him.

"And then?"

"He found a fissure some ways up." Alooma's crescent eyes filled with fear. "And Naidon, he's hurt."

Naidon's stomach tightened with dread as he remembered the feeder biting Sade's arm. He couldn't see whether the two feeders were still fighting outside, but he had to find Sade.

Naidon peeked his head out of the fissure. The two feeders were gone.

He and Alooma swam up three more levels before she pointed at an upcoming fissure in the wall. It was a tighter fit for her and especially for him—the Birthing Wall was for meeraids, the smallest of the maidoa types—but they both made it.

Sade was nowhere in sight. "Alooma, where is he—" At the back of the fissure, a small red figure huddled.

"Over there!" Alooma confirmed what Naidon had realized.

Sade was resting on the fissure bottom, cradling his arm. Deep gashes ran up from his wrist all the way to his shoulder. He'd lost a lot of blood. A few tears cluttered the corners of his elliptical eyes.

"Here, let me see?" Naidon approached slowly and reached out for his arm.

Sade yanked away. "Don't. Please . . ."

"I'm udon. We're healers."

"Maybe for your own pod, but not me."

"Naidon," Alooma's voice filled with concern. "You're hurt, too."

Sade stopped trying to look away and instead focused on Naidon's injury. The feeder's tooth had taken a small chunk out of Naidon's tail. He'd all but forgotten the pain until Alooma mentioned his injury.

"Let's see if I can heal us all." He noticed the scratches on Alooma's back from when that other udon had tried to force himself on her. "You're also in need of healing, Alooma."

"Oh." She seemed confused before she touched her back. "Yeah, guess with all that happened, I forgot all about it."

"I didn't," Naidon said. "Now go sit down beside Sade."

"Sade? You know his name?" Alooma sounded shocked. "When did you even have time to ask?"

Sade shook his head. "We didn't, which was why I thought it was weird that he asked."

"Well, I didn't want to keep calling you meeraid." Naidon smiled. "Now I know what to call you."

Sade studied him before looking away.

"Are you going to try to heal us or not?" Alooma sounded put out.

Naidon nodded. As an udon, one of his roles was to heal his pod. He didn't doubt that he'd be able to heal Alooma, but how would it go with Sade?

He let his instincts take over. In the same way that he could devour another udon, he could consume the injuries of his podmates. He wasn't sure what his body did with them, but he took them inside of him in the same way he did if he were to consume another udon.

When he opened his eyes, Alooma's scratches on her back were gone. Sade still had a small wound, but it was nothing like before.

His own tail looked the least healed, but he'd stopped the bleeding. That would have to be enough.

"You're still hurt?" Apparently, it wasn't enough for Alooma. "Can you try again?" She looked Sade over. "I can't believe you were even able to heal him. That's—"

"An excellent sign!" Naidon felt the first sense of peace. This gave him hope that they would be able to join. He shook off Alooma's worrying hands. "I'll be fine. After we join, I'll probably lose most of this length anyway, so it's okay." Juvenile udons became a lot smaller when they grew into adults.

This allowed them to live in the planet's air layers.

Sade got up and swam for the fissure exit.

"Wait! Where are you going?" Naidon said.

Sade looked over his shoulder. "What do you want?"

Naidon went after him, dragging Alooma along. "Want? It's almost time. If we don't all join, we won't be able to ascend to the Skies."

"Join?" Sade sounded a bit disgusted. "We're not a pod."

Alooma yanked her hand free. "Like I was saying all along, Naidon. This meeraid isn't one of us." Then she addressed Sade. "Where is your pod? Did you lose them?"

Sade shrugged. "I don't need one."

Naidon and Alooma looked at each other, taken aback.

"Oh?" Alooma snarled. "Just how are you planning on surviving in the ocean all by yourself, huh?"

"I'll manage."

She snorted. "Like you did with the feeders?"

"Alooma . . ." Naidon cautioned.

"If it wasn't for us," she continued. "You would be dinner right now."

Sade looked away before he mumbled. "Thanks." He gazed out at the open waters. "I'm not joining any pod."

"Sade—" Naidon started to say.

Alooma held up her hand. "Forget it. We can't make him join. And who knows, it might not be possible to join with him, even if he did want to."

"But the healing worked." Naidon looked Sade up and down. "Sure, it's not perfect, but the fact that I can means that it's possible. Besides, there were times when our pod lost a parental, of that much I know. All we need is to form a connection, and we'll be able to do it." He caught Sade's hand. "And we've formed one, even before I healed you. I know you've felt it, too."

"Huh?" Sade drawled out the word. "Connection? When

was this?"

"The moment we met. Don't you remember?"

"Met?" Alooma interrupted. "Naidon, you met him before?"

He nodded. "Yes. It was when"—he looked away—"we lost Laraid."

"Don't tell me you let Laraid die because of him?" Accusatory anger replaced the sadness in Alooma's eyes.

"I tried to save Laraid." Naidon hung his head, "But I failed."

Sade went to pull his hand away, but Naidon held on tight.

"That's when I saw you." Naidon's gaze softened. "We looked at each other. I felt it. As did you, I could see it in your eyes."

"Oh?" Sade snarled. "Was that when the feeders captured me and took me away? You're a real piece of work. Do you honestly think I was dreaming of you as they carried me off to be dinner?"

"I planned on coming back for you."

"You did what?" Alooma sounded even more betrayed.

"When?" Sade cut her off. "When they sliced me up?"

"I had to seek out my bolooa, but after that, I promised myself I would return for you."

Alooma backed away, shaking her head. "That's why you didn't fight me when I wanted to go looking for Laraid. I could call you a lot of things, but I never thought manipulative would be one of them."

Alooma knew Naidon's personality from their inherited parental memories, as he knew hers. A pang of guilt struck him. He'd never meant to let her down.

"Look," Naidon said to Sade. "I know I shouldn't have left you, but I made a calculated risk."

Alooma shoved Naidon, and his hand dislodged from Sade's. "Are you just going to ignore me?"

"I'm not trying to ignore you, dear Alooma. But we're running out of time. We need to join. Otherwise, we won't survive."

Alooma snorted. "And why would I want to join with a dishonest udon like you?"

"Alooma . . ."

When Naidon looked over to Sade, he was no longer there, the sliver of his tail exiting the fissure. "Come on. We have to catch him."

"No." Alooma glared at him. "I won't. If you wish to run out to your death in search of your new lover, by all means, I will be staying right here."

"And risk losing our chance to leave?"

"Leave? Leave to what? My meeraid is gone, and my udon is a traitorous deceiver. What do I have exactly?"

Naidon bowed his head. "I'm sorry, Alooma. I'd give my life for you a hundred times over—"

"And yet you didn't for Laraid? You just left him."

"He was gone. Devoured. And I needed to find you. Trust me when I say that it was the hardest decision I had to make yet."

"In what? In all your limited time alive? How touching." Alooma swam deeper into the fissure. "Leave me alone. Go and chase after your new meeraid, and while you're at it, go and find yourself another bolooa."

"I can't." Naidon went after her. "I can't live without you. I know that we've been joined longer than we were with our meeraid. That I know. Not that I didn't love him deeply. I did. I wish I could've saved him."

"Was he there?"

"Who?"

"The feeder who killed our mate. Was he in the village?"

"I don't know. They don't look all that different."

"Didn't you want revenge for Laraid?" Alooma appeared

to be remembering something. "And yet, when we were there, all of your focus was on saving that meeraid."

"That's because I had to think of the group, of you." Naidon tried to take her hand, but she didn't let him. Bolooas were natural diverters—one of the reasons she'd managed to escape that feeder. "It wouldn't have brought him back, Alooma."

"No, but it would've allowed him the peace of knowing that we loved him enough to seek justice for him."

"We would've died if we tried to do that."

"Then maybe we should've. He would have wanted us to go out together."

"You know he wouldn't have wanted that."

Alooma's shoulders shook and a few tears leaked from her crescent eyes, only to be carried off by the liquid mercury.

"Yes, when you decided to go to the feeders' village, I went with you, hoping to find Sade." Naidon bowed his head. "I'm sorry if I deceived you. Trust me when I say that you are the most important maidoa to me. I failed to save Laraid, but if you come with me, I promise I will spend the rest of my life making it up to you. Please." He offered his hand, his voice pleading. "For our lineage, our future offspring, and for Laraid, let's not die here, but become the pod we're meant to be."

Alooma cried a few more tears. Naidon wiped them away with his thumbs, being mindful of his claws.

She took his hand, and her porous skin connected with his. "Okay, let's go. But lie to me again and I will not follow you."

"Thank you, Alooma. I swear to you, I'll never do it again."

They swam to the edge of the fissure, and Naidon checked for feeders. The opaque water was blue enough to see. Nothing but a vast, empty ocean surrounded them.

His heart panged with dread. Sade! Where was he? What if the feeders had captured him? Worse yet . . . what if they had gobbled him up?

He hadn't lied about his connection with Sade. The idea of finding another meeraid repulsed him. He mourned the loss of Laraid, and if he hadn't spotted Sade, he would've felt the same as Alooma. But after meeting Sade, he knew in his heart that they belonged together, that Sade was the only meeraid he wanted.

"Can you sense him at all?" Alooma asked.

He and Sade weren't of the same pod. They weren't supposed to be able to sense one another. And yet . . . the link he'd felt with Sade was real.

Maybe he could try.

He closed his eyes and listened to the longing he felt, trying to sense the meeraid who'd captured his heart in the briefest moments when first they met.

With Alooma, as with their previous meeraid, Naidon had felt them instinctively, like they were parts of his own body. He knew where they were. It was as natural as breathing.

Not now.

The more he thought about Sade, the more his heart ached. He remembered the look in Sade's eyes when, for a fraction of time, they had stared at each other before the feeders carried him off.

Wonder? Attraction? Desire, maybe? And underneath a trace of familiarity, like they'd met before.

A memory of Sade resurfaced. The way his mouth twitched in a half smile before the feeders had snatched him. It didn't look like Sade's smile was something he had done on purpose. Then his expression was replaced by one of fear when the feeders had grabbed him.

A heady rush of protectiveness filled Naidon. He should have gone for Sade. Right then, right there. But Alooma had needed him. He'd felt her distress. Something had been threatening her, and he did what his instincts demanded and went for the female in his pod—his lover and podmate, whose heart he knew almost as well as his own. But a flicker of himself had never left Sade.

It was that part that Naidon searched for now. Their bond. Their spark. The tiny pieces of themselves that stayed with the other.

Got it!

It was faint but present.

Sade wasn't that far away. And he wasn't alone.

Feeders?

Naidon had no way of knowing. "This way! I found him!"

A look of disbelief crossed Alooma's face, but she moved with him in unison.

The water brightened the closer they approached, and he recognized Sade.

An udon and bolooa surrounded him.

"No! I won't join with you!" Sade yelled.

"But you're our mate," the bolooa said. Two of her tentacles snaked around Sade's arms, and they held him in place.

Sade shook his head. "I'm not. And you both know it."

The udon and bolooa pair must have lost their meeraid, and they were trying to catch another.

The udon ran his hand down Sade's chest, lightly scraping with his claws. Then he tipped Sade's chin up, holding him still. "Get on him," he called to the bolooa, who mounted Sade's back.

Her hands pressed into his chest, suction on her fingers sticking them together. The rest of her tentacles wrapped around his tail—some slithering up his torso.

"Get off!" Sade cried, but he didn't have the strength to dislodge her.

The udon cupped Sade's head, pressing them into each other. Sade cried out in what sounded like pain. The other two also hissed in apparent distress. The bolooa loosened her grip, nursing her wounds.

"This isn't working," she said to her udon.

"It will work." He wrapped his own tail around Sade's, attempting to merge their skin together. It must have also been painful, because the udon sucked in a breath, but he didn't stop.

Sade's head dropped onto the bolooa's shoulder. The udon nipped his exposed neck with his fangs.

"Get off me," Sade weakly protested.

They were trying to force a pod creation. Would it work? Naidon had no intention of waiting to find out.

He charged the udon, and the force dislodged the group, jettisoning Naidon and the udon out into the open water.

CHAPTER SEVEN: ALOOMA

Alooma languidly approached Sade and the other bolooa, sizing up her competition. Unlike Naidon, she didn't intend to fight. "He's not your meeraid, but ours," she said. "You will leave him alone."

"Or?" Drawing out the word, the other bolooa caught Sade in her tentacles again, pulling him until his face rested on her chest.

Sade began thrashing.

Alooma narrowed her crescent eyes into slits. "Or there will be consequences."

"Like what your udon is doing to mine?" The bolooa surveyed the two udons fighting—tails swiping, claws out, sharp fangs tearing into each other. "Mine'll win, you know?"

"Don't be so certain. It was my udon who felt a connection to this meeraid. That's how we were able to find him."

"This meeraid doesn't have a pod." The other bolooa's voice held flat certainty.

"He does now," Alooma said.

Something akin to sadness filled the other's crescent eyes, and her voice softened. "You both lost your meeraid, too. I understand your grief. But we also must survive."

"You can't join with him. A pod cannot be forced. Why not salvage the remaining time you have left to search for another meeraid?"

The bolooa stroked her long fingers through Sade's wispy hair. "This one's perfect, though."

"This one is ours." Alooma's voice hardened.

The bolooa scoffed. "You're welcomed to try and claim him, if you can."

"Is that a challenge?"

The other bolooa returned her smirk. She wrapped a tentacle around his torso, then snaked it down his abs. "I don't plan to release him."

"Then you leave me no choice." Alooma hugged Sade from behind, resting her head on his fin. Sade stilled at her touch. "That's it," she whispered into his ear, "Naidon was right about you. You *are* ours." She adjusted the bolooa's tentacle to gain access to his skin.

Sade leaned heavily into Alooma. "No. I'm free," he whispered. "I won't join with any pod." Alooma's tongue licked the shell of his pointy ear, and she tugged on his lobe with her fangs.

"Stop it," the other bolooa said, growling. "He's mine." She brought Sade up for a kiss, and she forced her tongue into his mouth, curling it around his.

Sade flailed against the bolooa and recoiled into Alooma's hold.

Alooma turned his head with a claw-tipped finger. The bolooa was still kissing him, and her head also turned at the motion. Alooma licked along their joined mouths. Sade's body began to respond at her touch, and he opened his mouth wider to allow Alooma to enter.

Alooma found the bolooa's tongue entrapping Sade's. She licked around it, drawing a moan from Sade.

Like she'd been struck, the other bolooa stopped kissing him. "No," she whispered. "You can't take him. I won't let you."

Alooma continued to work Sade's mouth open, her tongue massaging his, drawing moan after moan from his throat.

He reached a hand behind him and tangled his webbed fingers in the plumes of her hair.

The other bolooa ran her tentacles over Sade's chest, all the way down to his tail, tracing along his skin, and he shivered, dropping the kiss between him and Alooma.

Alooma growled. She snaked her own tentacles down Sade's spine, wrapping around his body, overlapping the bolooa's and forcing her way to make direct contact with Sade. Her jelly-like skin massaged Sade's pores. She ran her hands down his chest, feeling the contours of his tight muscles. Slowly, her hand began to dissolve into his body, and for a moment, they melded into one flesh.

The other bolooa had little success trying to merge with Sade. She pressed hard, but his skin didn't give way no matter how she touched him.

Having recovered from the other bolooa's interruption, Sade looked over his shoulder and met Alooma's lips again. His tongue ran along the seam before she gave him access. He touched her hair plumes until his fingers melded again with her tentacles.

The other bolooa released Sade and moved back.

Alooma was now free to encircle Sade completely in her tentacles and hold him close.

Shaking her head, the other bolooa whispered, "This isn't over. We desire this meeraid, and we will have him, in this cycle or another."

Alooma smirked and pivoted Sade until he faced her. She was taller and more massive, so from one direction, Sade couldn't be seen. "That will never happen. Now call off your udon. You still have time to find yourself a meeraid, but not for much longer."

The other bolooa looked over to her udon. Alooma did, too. Sade seemed too busy nuzzling against Alooma's soft skin. His tail moved in the gentle flow of the water, getting lost in the feel of her tentacles around him. His pores opened to hers, and where they touched, they dissolved into her.

The udons were still fighting, but Alooma was right, and Naidon had the upper hand. But the other udon didn't back down, both aware of their dire situation. From the way he fought, he, too, strongly desired Sade, who now began to kiss along Alooma's shoulder and up her throat.

"It's over," the other bolooa said to her udon.

Both udons separated, still glaring at each other. The other udon abruptly left, swimming to his bolooa's side. "Are you sure?" he asked.

His bolooa nodded sadly. "It's no use. She's got him. I couldn't compete."

"Well then, we've got no choice." He leveled Naidon with a death glare. "This isn't over. I promise you, be it in the Skies or the Harvests, we will find you and take back what we claimed. Perhaps my bolooa couldn't take him over, but he was yielding to me. If you hadn't arrived, it would have only been a matter of time before he surrendered."

Naidon squared his shoulders. "Until we meet again. And once we do, I'll make you regret trying to force yourself on him."

The other bolooa scoffed. "So high and mighty when you both seek to do the same." Then she and her udon swam off until they were lost in the opaque waters.

Chapter Eight: Sade

Sade exhaled Alooma's sweet scent, and the fear lurking in the pits of his stomach dissipated. He'd almost been sucked into that other bolooa and udon's pod. If things felt stifling with Naidon and Alooma, it had been much, much worse with that other pair.

Now comparing Naidon to the previous udon, he looked taller. Fitter. Stronger. Far more handsome than Sade remembered. And there was something else. Some other primal call beckoned to Sade, rooting him in place. Perhaps he was in too deep.

"We're running out of time," Naidon said, nearing them.

Alooma still had her tentacles wrapped around Sade, holding him against her breasts. Slowly, she nodded. "Come on, let's join."

Sade shivered at that. A part of him still wanted to be free, without a pod, without lovers to trap him. Sluggishly, he pushed away from her. "No. I must be free."

Naidon crowded him from behind. He ran his fingers through Sade's hair in a loving, tender motion. "It's all right. You'll see. We're made for this. For unity, connection."

Alooma released Sade and moved back. "What happened to your pod?"

Sade tried to shove down his shame. "It doesn't matter."

"It does to me." She looked at Naidon longingly. An undertone of a question lay in her voice as if she wasn't quite sure Naidon felt the same. "To us."

"I never found them, nor did I want to."

"Alooma," Naidon said, his tone both compassionate and urgent. "We can talk about this later. The Skies are calling. It's now or never."

"But don't you want to know? Some pod is without a meeraid and possibly dying as a result. Do we really want to join with someone so selfish?"

"Can you still feel them?" Naidon spoke near Sade's ear.

Sade didn't even want to try. What was it that made him feel so distant from his pod? He'd thought it was his need for independence, but now he wasn't so sure. Nothing told him to shun his own kin . . . and yet. Something lurked in his parental memories that prevented him from connecting with them.

He shook his head in response to Naidon's question.

"Perhaps they died before he could reach them?" Naidon said to Alooma.

She released a sigh. "I don't trust this."

"And yet, you two were able to merge. This feels right, and I know it does to you, too."

Alooma ran her webbed fingers down Sade's chest, and her mesoglea skin began sticking to his. A soft smile graced her face. "I *do* feel it." She used her tentacles to pull him closer until he rested his head on her breasts. Her heart pitter-pattered against his ear. Long plumes on her waist wrapped around him, and her tentacles crawled down his tail, tantalizing his fin that ran the length of his body and was extra sensitive.

He sighed and trailed his hands up her back. His webbed fingers began to meld into her body as he kissed down her neck and over her breasts, her nipples peaking as he teased them with his fangs.

Using her tentacles, she brought him up for a kiss, slow and deep.

Naidon's muscular chest pressed into Sade's back, bending

Sade's flexible fin until it lay flat against Naidon's abs. Unlike Alooma's, Naidon's hide was rough and grainy, but as their bodies prepared to merge, it started to soften.

Sade shivered as Naidon whispered into his ear, "It's time." A thrill of excitement ran up his spine.

When Alooma released his mouth and kissed over his cheeks and eyelids, Naidon cupped Sade's chin and made him look over his shoulder. Slowly, he fitted their lips together.

Sade trembled as energy and heat shot through him. This *did* feel right—all of it.

He parted his lips at Naidon's pressing tongue and allowed him to enter. Far more forceful than Alooma, Naidon's kiss demanded everything from him, even his very soul.

Alooma grazed his neck, nipping with her fangs, kissing along his throat. Sade trailed his fingers over her torso and up the curves of her body to her breasts. She pressed into him, and his skin gave way, and it was like he was inside her.

And he was.

Her plumes, long and golden, surrounded him. Her body curved, and her lower tentacles—the ones rougher and more squid-like—enclosed him and Naidon entirely, bringing them into their own world where no light could enter.

Sade could only feel.

Naidon hugged Alooma tightly, his webbed fingers clutched her backside, and Sade experienced Naidon's touch as if Sade were her. All the while, Naidon pressed behind him. Sade rested his head on Naidon's broad chest. Naidon made Sade look over his shoulder so he could kiss him.

Alooma licked along their joined mouths. Sade opened his completely, letting Alooma enter as well. Her tongue encircled his while Naidon's tongue explored his mouth. Alooma moaned, and it reverberated down Sade's throat.

Naidon circled Alooma's tongue, trapping Sade between

them.

It happened slowly. Naidon dissolved into him until he could feel the softness of Alooma's tentacles on Naidon's back. Her fingers massaged Naidon's scalp, making Naidon's sensitive fin feel amazing.

Alooma's waist plumes ran along Naidon's strong back and stroked his dorsal fin, and Sade could feel every touch Alooma gave Naidon.

Then her fingers found Sade's and brought them palm to palm.

Sade sensed it in his blood. They were about to merge. He felt a strong need to connect with his new lovers and newly emerging family.

Naidon covered Sade's hand with his larger one, his skin still tougher than Alooma's gelatin. The need to connect grew stronger. Sade's body tingled as he released the pheromone that allowed the join to happen. Without a meeraid, while bolooas and udons could meld a little, it was not possible for a maidoa join to occur.

All three of their hands pressed together. Sade acted as a medium between them, joining their bodies until they converged into a single being. He could feel them as if no barriers existed, and he couldn't tell where he ended, and they began. This oneness was unlike anything he'd experienced. Nothing in his parental memories had prepared him for this kind of intensity—to become completely one with others.

A strong taste filled the water. It was Naidon's essence. It was poisonous to feeders, which was why once a maidoa pod formed, feeders could no longer prey upon them. It also served to strip away the parts of their juvenile bodies no longer needed as adults.

Alooma's rough tentacles were the first to dissolve. Sade could see all 360 degrees around him, as now only her predominantly see-through plumes still held them together.

Slowly, they floated to the surface. Feeders swam in the waters below. Their jaws still opened, but they no longer chased them. Now they looked like any other harmless creature. It seemed ages ago that Sade had almost become their dinner.

Chapter Nine: Naidon

Naidon moaned, deep inside his lovers. His body was no longer his own, and yet, his entirely. He'd never been more complete than at this moment.

Alooma dissolved into him—her soft and warm plumes, jelly-like skin, essence, scent, taste, everything that was her had now become him.

And Sade. He felt like uncharted territory, and it made Naidon want, crave, desire.

He burned inside, forcing Sade to take all he had to offer, knowing he consumed Sade in a fire of passion that was new to Sade and new to Alooma, too.

Since he was one with both of them, he knew what they were feeling.

Newness.

Was this because Sade came from another pod?

Flashes of memories sparked in his mind. It was of his parentals joining, and it felt as real as if he'd been there—he, Alooma, and their meeraid. But it wasn't the meeraid in his arms. It must've been their previous one, Laraid. A jolt of sadness hit him hard, and all three of them cried out. Alooma's pain echoed his own, Sade experiencing it for seemingly the first time.

None of Sade's parental memories surfaced, and that should've been odd, but Naidon was fixated on the sensations in his body and mind—the rush of heat, familiarity, bonding, and love. The more they joined, the stronger and more intense these feelings became. And also, the higher they ascended through the oceanic layers, but again, Naidon's focus wasn't on their environment.

Feelings of burning, consuming fire—yet not of actual pain—dominated his being, and he melted into the fervor, lost on the high of his lovers and companions for life. *Sensory overload!* He exploded in a beautiful release, and the juvenile pieces of himself and his pod burst into the skies.

CHAPTER TEN: SADE

Sade was stripped to his core, overwhelmed by the sensations of joining with his podmates, but a fragment of his mind stayed his own. It was this part of him that kept him conscious of the world around him. He'd watched as they floated higher and higher, feeling the denser parts of themselves being stripped away, until they had ascended out from the layers of the ocean and into the air. They'd traveled all the way to one of the topmost atmospheric levels above the planet, where it dissolved into outer space.

Naidon and Alooma still enclosed him, but he could feel them returning to their separate entities. He didn't want them to leave, liking the feeling of fullness. Of unity. Togetherness. It was funny, given how much he'd fought it, but now he didn't want it ever to go away.

He registered their last bits of awareness as if Alooma's and Naidon's bodies were still his—chilly air nipped Naidon's skin as he drew in a deep breath of the misty nitrogen. His gills fluttered, taking in the moisture, feeling the coolness awake his lungs. A light breeze trembled over Alooma's webbed fingers as she reached up at the soft clouds with blackness behind them dotted with stars.

Then Sade was himself again. He felt substantially lighter and smaller. Alooma and Naidon had always been taller than him, but now neither was as massive. They looked different, more handsome, freer. Both were rather wispy. It would allow them to float through the less dense air.

Naidon's long tail still ended in a flipper, but now two

glossy plumes fanned out and flowed in the air. His dorsal fin still extended from the crown of his head to the middle of his back, although it was much less defined. He was still a brilliant shade of onyx, and his circular eyes also remained jet black. His broad shoulders and muscular physique were every bit as beautiful, but his skin was no longer coarse.

Alooma had changed, too. Her body was no longer as circular, and her torso was slenderer. Her plumes still made her look puffy. Having shed her juvenile shape, she was smaller, and plumes had replaced her lower body tentacles. The ones still on her head flowed in the air. Her larger crescent eyes filled out her face nicely. Their pale color, no longer amber, was almost lost in the sky around them. Her chest moved up and down as she breathed, and her breasts still looked inviting.

This was them as adults, and they were more desirable than ever.

Chapter Eleven: Alooma

Alooma reached out for Naidon, who pressed their palms together, fingers still webbed and ending with claws. Sade came close to them, and they opened their arms to allow him to get in the middle.

Alooma leaned her forehead against Naidon's, pressing her body into Sade. He was still smaller than Naidon and herself, so she could look over Sade into Naidon's eyes, still circular and jet black, like the space above them. Naidon was not as broad as he'd been in the watery substance below. His body was lighter and could move freely through the misty air, but he still took up space. His cranial fin wasn't as defined and was skinnier than when he was a juvenile.

Sade's face was the most beautiful with his newness. Alive, radiant, and pearly, but still red like the rest of his skin. His ruby elliptical eyes were narrower. His nose, formerly slits needed to help breathe underwater, had taken full shape. His ribbon-like body still had a flabby fin that ran from his head to the top of his tail. But now he was slenderer and moved more fluidly. He was a little bit smaller in size, but he fit nicely between her and Naidon.

They were a family, a pod, now. And yet, she knew so little about Sade. Thankfully, they would have some time to connect. Hopefully that would give them the time they needed to build enough of a connection to make it through the harvests—even when their memories were hidden to allow them to absorb the cultures and DNA of the planets on their mission—and so be able to return home and restart the cycle.

Of course, there was always a chance that the Collective would not assign her pod to work as Gatherers. But as she came from generations of Gatherers, Alooma doubted it.

The air around them was light, and so was her body. No longer held down by the long tentacles, even her plumes were finer. Releasing her podmates, she twirled about, reaching out at the open sky to the blankets of outer space, only a few layers of atmosphere above. That was when she spotted it. What looked like giant bubbles lined the horizon. The sunlight made their tops gleam like marbles.

Home.

Inside, their parentals were waiting.

Naidon and Sade were staring at each other. Sade wore an expression that Alooma couldn't place. Was he nervous? He looked like he'd just woken up from a dream.

"Come on." She took Naidon's slightly larger hand. Looking at their still webbed fingers, she brought them up to her lips and pressed kisses to them. "Let's go and find our parentals." Then she turned to Sade and reached out for his hand. "You, too."

"But aren't they not my parentals?" That was a weird way for Sade to phrase it.

"They are now." Alooma squeezed his hand—still webbed fingers like hers and Naidon's.

"Before we can do that, we must go to be counted," Naidon said, taking Sade's other hand. "Come on." Their plumes propelled them through the air as they had in the waters below.

As they approached, the bubbles grew large enough to block out the sun. The longer they stayed in the open air, the darker and colder it became.

Pods of maidoa were arriving from all directions. Would they see the bolooa and udon that tried to claim Sade? Had that pod managed to find a meeraid in time? Maybe not. Perhaps they were stuck as juveniles.

The entrances to the main bubble in the center had gathered quite the line. They were waiting to be registered and given their destined jobs. They came from a long line of parentals who had been Gatherers that went out on Harvests to bring back information and collect genes to their colony's epicenter, the Collective.

"Naidon." She looked at the long lines. "Maybe we should first go and visit our parentals, because who knows how long we'll have to wait."

Naidon sighed. "I guess more of maidoa survived than I thought. You're right. Perhaps we should go see them first."

This would be their first time ever meeting their three parentals, but it didn't feel like that. Rather, it felt like they were coming back from a Harvest. She and Naidon knew most things about their parentals' lives—the Harvests they went on, the genes and cultural traits they brought back.

But Sade did not.

Glancing at Sade, she found him staring around with wide eyes. Hadn't he had memories of their home world? If so, why was he acting like all of this was new?

"Well, let's go." Naidon took the lead as usual. "Our parentals are back from their Harvest. Right?" Most parentals were waiting for their offspring to become adults. They normally would not resume their work, whatever trade they might be in, until after they'd met their children. This was especially true for Gatherers, who would postpone their next Harvest.

Chapter Twelve: Sade

Sade followed rather reluctantly. They entered through a wide opening in the main bubble, bypassing the line that waited to meet the Collective and be assigned a job.

He could sense the excitement and urgency from his two podmates. Both looked forward to seeing their parentals. But Sade wasn't their biological son. How would they take to him?

Inside, rows of smaller bubbles lined. Some floated off to the side, while others stuck to the ceiling of the giant bubble. Maidoa pods moved through the air—tentacles propelling them forward. They conversed or played. Some even argued amongst each other.

The hunters had returned with their day's catch. Sade smirked when he saw a small feeder being strung up by its tail, mouth open, eyes lifeless.

He scoffed. It was dead, and he was alive. Of course, Sade had Naidon and Alooma to thank for that, not himself.

Off to the side, a few more pods approached. These maidoas were healers coming to see to any hunters who had been injured.

Sade wondered what it would be like to be working in either profession. They'd only know where they were assigned after they saw the Collective.

From joining with Naidon and Alooma, Sade knew they came from a long line of Gatherers. The most desired profession.

If he searched his own parental memories, he also found

those of gathering. But whenever he tried, a splitting pain filled his mind. He didn't want to press further. Something had happened in his parentals' cycles, and he had no desire to find out more, not if it would be a painful process.

He could no longer feel his bolooa like he could when he was first born. He didn't think he'd ever sensed his udon. Maybe he just never got close enough? He felt even more detached from his udon, also an undercurrent of something else—fear. Somewhere in his parental memories was a fear of his udon mate. *No. I don't even want to know.* Quickly, Sade shut his mind off to his memories.

Chapter Thirteen: Naidon

Naidon led the group. He took Alooma's and Sade's hands.

He recognized their parentals' dwelling—a medium-sized bubble whose outside was too opaque to see through. He knew they would be waiting for their children.

Excitement, and something else, filled his stomach—guilt.

He was coming home without the meeraid birthed by his parentals. How would they react?

They swam through the bubble, feeling the condition of the air change. Upon entering the house, he remembered all his parentals' names.

The house was also in 3-D space, with several sky plants hanging on the ceiling. A layer of curtains led into the back. But his attention was drawn to the three maidoas sitting on several cushions. He immediately recognized his udon father, Adon.

All three rose from their seats.

"My children!" His bolooa mother, Gelooma, rushed over to them. She threw her arms around them, drawing the three of them together.

Adon approached. So did Oamaid, their meeraid parental.

Adon put his hand on Naidon's head and smiled. "I'm glad you're all safe and home."

"Wait . . ." Oamaid spoke softly. "Where is Laraid?" Naidon flinched at the name of his original meeraid podmate.

Both Gelooma and Adon backed off so that all three could look at their children.

"No . . ." Several tears leaked from the corner of Gelooma's crescent eyes. Unlike in the ocean, the air current wasn't strong enough to carry tears away. Instead, they sparkled in the setting sunlight.

Naidon bowed his head. "Forgive me, my parentals." He directed his gaze first to Oamaid, then Gelooma, and finally Adon. "I tried to save him, but I was too late."

Adon's eyes narrowed—jet black like his own. It was more than apparent that Naidon was this parental's clone. "And yet, you failed."

"Now wait just a second!" Alooma's voice held anger that he hadn't heard before. "Where were you all when we were in the ocean below? We needed your help. And yet, none of you came. And you have the nerve to blame Naidon? If it weren't for him, I would have been kidnapped by another udon, probably forced to join with him or die. And then, after we lost Laraid, I wanted to give up, but Naidon didn't let me."

Adon's eyes narrowed.

"What?" Alooma said. "Did you wish to lose all of your children?"

"Alooma . . ." Naidon cautioned.

"No, I'm not finished. After we joined, I saw all Naidon's memories. I saw how hard he tried to save Laraid. All the pain he felt when he couldn't. You don't know what it was like, so don't you dare judge us!"

"Calm down, my child." Their bolooa parent, Gelooma, spoke in a softer voice. "You have no idea how much we wished to come and help you children. But— "

"It's not how things are done." Alooma cut her off. "I know, but that means you all need to cut Naidon some slack. He risked everything." She looked at her two podmates. "We all did. And somehow, we survived."

Gelooma hugged them again—all three of them, Sade included. "I'm sorry it was so painful."

Adon and Oamaid were silent.

Naidon tried to read their expressions.

Sadness. That was what he saw in Oamaid's red elliptical eyes.

Then Oamaid nodded and swam into the room behind the veil—where they slept.

Adon studied his children for a second more. "I understand it was hard. It was the same for us. Excuse me." He headed after Oamaid.

Naidon's chest ached. What if he had to comfort Alooma, or Sade, after the loss of a child? How could he be upset at Adon's behavior? After all, Naidon would die inside if he had to watch his lovers suffer like that.

Alooma relaxed at his side. "I'm sorry, we didn't mean to upset them. But what I said was true, and I don't regret that." That she'd been able to speak her mind like that was truly amazing.

"Forgive me." He bowed his head to Gelooma. "I'm sorry I failed." And he was. But inside, doubts filled his mind. Had he been able to save Laraid, he wouldn't have Sade standing by his side. Feeders would have devoured Sade.

Naidon's heart was torn. Of course, he wanted to save Laraid. But he couldn't deny losing Sade would be equally troubling, maybe even more. And that filled him with shame.

Chapter Fourteen: Sade

Sade had never felt more uncomfortable and unwanted. What was he doing here? He wasn't the meeraid the parentals were expecting. What would that mean for him and the future with his pod?

Gelooma, now his bolooa mother as well, looked over at him. "What is your name?" That was right. She hadn't named him, so she didn't know it. Each type of maidoa was named by their type's parental. Sade had been named by his meeraid parental. In the same way, Naidon had been by his udon parental, and Alooma her bolooa parental.

"Sade," he said, wondering about the meeraid parental who had named him. Was some other meeraid out there grieving his lost child? Sade didn't feel sad. Nor did he miss them. What in the world happened that made him so detached from them? He might be able to find out if he let himself remember, but he couldn't.

"Sade," Gelooma repeated his name as if trying it out. "What happened to your pod, do you know?"

"No." He spoke truthfully. What had become of them he didn't know, and he honestly didn't care, but he wasn't about to tell his new mother that.

"I'm sorry to hear that you lost them. But now you are my new son, Sade. Please feel welcome here."

That almost made him smile, but he could only give half of one. "Um, thanks."

As evening started to settle in, the family gathered for dinner.

They were having feeder stew, and Sade was going to savor every last bit of it. *Now, look who's dinner?*

Alooma must've seen him smile, for she grinned at him. "This looks amazing." She directed the compliment to her parentals.

"They were freshly caught today," Oamaid replied. He looked like he had cheered up a bit. Sade still needed to speak with him one on one, and he wasn't looking forward to it.

His new udon parental, Adon, silently ate his food. When he finally spoke, it stole Sade's attention. "Will you be getting processed tomorrow? Or have you already done so?"

"We came straight here," Naidon responded. "Tomorrow we will go."

Processed. That word irked Sade. He wished he hadn't stopped swimming when he first saw Naidon fighting. That thought saddened him, and it was both puzzling and scary. The former because, given his aloofness to his own pod, it was strange that he didn't feel similarly to his new one. Instead, he felt a connection with them, especially to Naidon. And that scared him because even now, after he'd been forced to join or die, Sade still wanted to remain his own maidoa.

After dinner, Oamaid approached him. "May I have a moment?"

Sade nodded and followed him outside of the bubble to what looked like a patio. The wind dragged their bubble farther down into the atmosphere, so it would be harder to float, but here there was some flooring, so he sat down next to Oamaid.

Heavy silence engulfed them. Sade had no idea what to say and wished he could go back inside.

"Do you not want to be here?" Oamaid said.

Sade wasn't expecting him to speak, and it startled him. "Why do you say that?"

"As a meeraid, I can tell more of what you're feeling, since

I can understand your facial expressions better than the others can."

"Oh . . ." Sade scratched his neck with his claws. Oamaid was half correct. "It's not like I don't want to be here. It's just all so new." *And weird and uncomfortable and very unwelcoming.*

"Have you really no idea what became of your pod?"

Gelooma must have spoken to Oamaid about this because only she had asked Sade about his pod.

"No, not really."

"But you had them. Did you leave them, or was it the other way around?"

"Why does it matter?"

"It matters because you will be living with my children now, and your actions will either save them or else put them at risk."

Sade knew all of this, but what did this other meeraid want him to say? He still wasn't even sure what he thought about it.

"I know," he finally ended up saying.

"You are the substance that holds the pod together. It is only with you present that they can fully join. You must be aware of the responsibility that you hold to the group. And as my son, my new son, I won't let you put the others at risk."

"We're already joined," Sade said. "Not much can be done about it now."

Oamaid scoffed. "I knew there was something about you that I didn't like." He shook his head, and his hair tentacles flowed in the soft wind. "But I want to give you a chance. It's not your fault my true son is dead."

"Um, thank you." Sade didn't know what else to say. He didn't want to start on bad terms with his meeraid parental. After all, they were going to spend the rest of their long lives together.

"Just remember how important you are to them. Never

forget that. And you should all be okay."

Chapter Fifteen: Naidon

The next day, Naidon and his pod headed over to be processed. As they waited in line, which wasn't as long as the previous day, Naidon pondered what to do.

The Collective would assign them to one of the four possible professions. The first were Hunters. They provided food for the colony by hunting in the oceans below. Some also tended to crops, either air or water based. Without Hunters, everyone would starve. As jobs went, they were essential.

The second were Healers. These pods helped maintain the health of the colony. Mostly they existed to heal any injured Hunter.

The third profession, and the one he wanted to belong to, was the Gatherers. He and Alooma came from a long line of these. Most of their parental memories had been honed as such. If they wanted all that information to continue onto their children, their pod needed to be in the same profession. Otherwise, while their offspring would have some memories, they would be more general and make them less proficient. In some ways, it would be as if their parentals' efforts didn't matter.

"What are you thinking, Naidon?" Alooma asked.

Naidon shook his head. "We can't end up as Caregivers."

Caregivers were the last profession. They took care of the colony. Some maidoa looked down upon them, since they didn't add to the Collective as Gatherers did, nor did they risk their lives like Hunters.

But new pods were often assigned to be Caregivers first.

Then a few cycles later, they were allowed into other professions. But by then, all their parentals' efforts would be lost.

"Better that than end up falling apart," Alooma said.

The line moved quickly, and soon, only one more pod was in front of them.

Naidon looked to Sade, who was staring out at the horizon. Most likely, Alooma was right. It would be too risky to take on another job other than a Caretaker. However much he loved Sade, Naidon had to admit that Sade had a wild spirit. But their pod still shared a connection. That had to count, right?

"Next pod, please." The three maidoa at the gate were a Caretaker pod. They were surely dedicated to their work, but not in Naidon's eyes. To him, they appeared bored, unfulfilled, shamed.

Not all maidoa felt this way, and certainly not those from long lines of parental Caretakers, but Naidon and his pod were different. If they weren't Gatherers, then what was the point of their existence?

"Come on." Naidon grabbed Sade's hand, shaking him out of his apparent daze. He reached for Alooma, who put her hand in his.

"Nice form," the udon member of the Caretaker pod said. "All move in unison."

From the corner of his eye, Naidon thought he saw Sade bristle.

The Caretaker udon led them up a path through the air high above the surface of the bubble.

"Now, udon leader," he said. "Step forward."

Naidon complied. He stood in front of his podmates but hadn't released their hands.

"You are the leader of the group. Do you vouch for their loyalty?"

He could feel Alooma's gaze on him. What was she

expecting him to say?

"Yes, I do."

"And how long have you been a pod?"

Naidon returned to his parental memories. He searched for the different links that each generation of his parentals provided.

"Seven parental joinings."

Alooma's eyes widened, but she didn't say anything. She knew that Naidon hadn't included Sade in all of this.

The udon caretaker studied them, and his unibrow rose. "Seven, huh?"

Naidon nodded, schooling his emotions and trying to come off as confident.

He wondered what Sade felt about all of this, but it would only give them away if he tried to look at him.

"And your line are Gatherers, correct?"

Naidon nodded.

"You may attempt to proceed with the profession of Gatherer. Now, go before the Collective."

The udon Caretaker directed them to a path leading into the heart of the bubble.

Alooma squeezed his hand and lingered. "What are you doing, Naidon?"

"Please, trust me on this."

"Trust? You do realize that you could get us killed by doing this?" Alooma glared. "A few cycles of Caretaker work would allow our pod to bond."

"And what about our parentals?" More guilt washed over Naidon. "Everything they taught us will be for nothing."

"Not necessarily." Alooma bunched her brow. "Please don't tell me you're willing to put your pride before the life of our pod?"

"Not pride." Naidon's voice turned sad.

"Then guilt?" Alooma cupped his face. "Naidon, you tried

your best. Adon can't be upset with you."

"But he is. I have shamed him."

"Forget that!" Fire blazed in Alooma's crescent, opal eyes. "We need to move forward with our own pod. Not live under our parentals' wishes—" Alooma's mouth fell open.

Ahead was a large glowing sphere.

The Collective.

They had never laid eyes on it, other than in their parental memories.

"Woah . . ." Naidon whispered.

A Caregiver pod blocked off entry into the sanctuary housing the Collective. They opened their mouths and spoke in a single voice in different octaves. "Maidoa pod—Naidon, Alooma, and Sade—join with the Collective and know your role."

Naidon led his pod into the sanctuary.

The Collective rested in the center. The glowing bluish-opalescent sphere was so high that he couldn't see the top. He remembered the mountainous sphere and how it hummed and vibrated as they approached, but parental memories paled in comparison to real life. Tendrils of electricity made the pores on his skin tingle. With each step towards the Collective, hundreds of little voices could be heard whispering.

The source of all the maidoa power. Inside lay a treasure-trove of knowledge, customs, sensations, culture, DNA, and features harvested by the maidoa from a plethora of planets.

Now it was their turn.

All maidoa could take from the Collective. To some degree, all could add to the Collective, too, but not in the way Gatherers could. To see what profession their pod would be assigned to, they would be tested before the Collective. If they could take from its knowledge and give back to it at a high enough level, they would become Gatherers.

But they were a new pod now because of Sade. Maidoa

could only gather or receive information from the Collective as a pod, not individually. When the Collective took from them, it would be taxing and all but impossible in weak or fresh pods that lacked cycles of bonding and experiences inherited from their parentals. So, if the pod did not proceed as a unit, they were doomed to fail.

All this Naidon knew, but he hoped they could become Gatherers. Otherwise, every cycle of experience their parentals had acquired could be diluted with ones where they worked another profession, and Naidon had already disappointed his udon parental enough.

Alooma put her back to the sphere, and Naidon and Sade took either side of her until they formed a triangle. Naidon held up his palms and waited for his podmates. Alooma pressed hers against his. Sade hesitated but did the same. Then Alooma and Sade joined palms, completing the triangle.

Naidon closed his eyes, letting the presence of his two podmates fill his senses. Alooma shone like a beacon beside him. He could feel her every sensation, like how the Collective smelled differently to her than him. Sade, however, was shrouded in silence. Naidon focused on the tiny connection that drew him and Sade together, the spark that had blossomed long before the three of them had joined. Sade's fingers began to meld into his. As soon as that happened, Alooma and his hands blended together as well.

Their bodies merged into a single, floating entity that pressed into the sphere.

Like a wave that rushed over them, Naidon felt submerged by the Collective. Inside were emotions, sensations, and experiences alien to themselves, but memories resurfaced upon hearing and feeling them.

Every sensation could be seen as a figment, and when he reached out for it, it became a part of him. Laughter rippled through them. A race expressed their happiness this way.

Now he and his pod could do likewise.

Something that looked like squiggles moved across his vision. *Language*. It belonged to another race on a planet visited by maidoa long ago. His tongue curled and whacked his pallet as he spoke the newly learned words. Then hundreds of languages surrounded him, all from the many cultures returned to the Collective.

He could experience how the Collective made him feel and how his podmates experienced the Collective as they were still of one mind.

Alooma was in awe. She inhaled a heavenly scent from a puffy cloud. *Sweetness*. At first, she hadn't known what to call it, but upon smelling it, she learned.

One culture had numerous ways to see, not just from their eyes but fingers and foreheads. Sade was afraid at first as his new senses awoke. He seemed to have an underlying bit of fear in his parental memories. It made Naidon even more curious as to Sade's past. But unlike his connection with Alooma, he could only sense so much from Sade, and his past was the most elusive.

Naidon could still feel his physical body even while inside his pod's joined body, and it was also changing. Along his dorsal fin, soft hair follicles grew until he had a full head of black hair—just like his udon father, Adon. Naidon welcomed it, savoring all the brilliance that being part of the Collective entailed. Being one with the Collective was so enjoyable that Naidon didn't want to leave it, and the exact time that passed was lost to him. It could have been mere seconds, but he felt like he'd experienced centuries of realities. It felt like coming home. Like he was finally one with his species.

But none of what they were doing made them Gatherers. They were retrieving information from the Collective, not adding to it.

It was time to see if they were truly Gatherers.

The Collective entered them, and it was like they were being submerged into the ocean. Heaviness and fluids filled his gills. The world came into focus, and he found himself in his pod's shared mind. When a pod joined, they essentially became one being, and so they shared a mind. Inside that mind, though, they were represented as glowing versions of their physical selves.

Energy shot forth from Naidon's palms. Blue and glowing, it connected with identical energies coming from Alooma's and Sade's hands. Again they formed a triangle, joined by these energy beams.

The line between him and Alooma was rich, strong, and perfectly straight. Between him and Sade, however, it bowed inward, but not nearly as concave as the one between Sade and Alooma.

Realization dawned on Naidon. These beams represented their bonds with each other. It also confirmed something that Naidon had been pondering. While Sade and Alooma's bond did exist between them, a good portion of it channeled through their separate relationships with Naidon.

At the very center of their triangle, a tiny blue sphere glowed, looking no bigger than a teardrop. The Collective. It was inside their shared mind. It was time to see if they could contribute to it at the level that was required for all Gatherers.

As a bolooa, Alooma's desire to enhance the Collective burned strong, and Naidon would be spilling his heart out to the Collective, if not for Sade, who lagged behind. However strong Alooma's willpower, if Sade weren't a Gatherer, they would be blocked.

Naidon knew what to do. Some of the information they would be sharing would be their experiences as juveniles. Naidon focused on how he met his podmates, how they struggled to survive, how he loved them. He remembered how they lost their original meeraid, Laraid, and his heart ached.

Alooma and Sade cried out in pain as well.

A wave of healing sprang up, coming from their new meeraid, Sade. Naidon and Sade's bond soothed the hurt and filled the emptiness with peace and joy. Alooma blew out a breath, clearly feeling the warmth of their connection.

Sade released a shaky sigh. Naidon sensed that he was astounded by the sensation of togetherness. A joining between a pod that took place in the Collective was the most intimate experience in a maidoa's lifetime. What had happened to Sade's parental memories that made him lack such events?

Each pod member also needed to recall their parental memories for their specific type. So Naidon was to recall all his udon parental's memories, while Alooma was to do the same to their bolooa parental. And finally, Sade needed to recall the memories from his own meeraid parental.

Naidon opened himself up and focused on the memories he was born with, giving them all his attention. He thought about his udon father and the many life cycles he had led. While he did have parental memories of his other maidoa parentals, mostly they came from when they joined as a pod. He had memories from his ancestors as well, although they were more distant.

All around their shared mind, images and sensations flashed—the memories that Naidon recalled. Other memories flickered, too, colors, places, and feelings of closeness. These must have been Alooma's projection of their bolooa's parental memories.

Sade lagged behind. None of his memories were present.

Of their pod, Alooma held the strongest link to the Collective. At her call, tiny fragments of Sade's parental memories began to depict on the walls as well. He *had* been a Gatherer. Feelings of togetherness, of strength, filled their shared space.

The Collective grew as it gorged on the memories that

flashed all around it. As they continued, not only did the Collective swell, but the beams between them became stronger and more intense until their triangle shined in a blinding light.

Splintering pain and fear laced through Sade's connection, and an ugly red color splattered over their memories. It burned their eyes and hurt all the way down to their core. Sade cried out, and any memory that he was providing stopped.

The Collective wavered.

Oh no.

Depositing toxicity was forbidden, and the Collective would not take from a negative place.

Something inside Sade's memories must be causing him distress. The beams connecting Sade and Alooma collapsed inward, and they would have collided completely if not for the Collective inside the triangle.

The Collective shrieked and groaned. Teetering, it stopped growing.

The ray connecting Naidon to Sade also bowed, not as much as Sade and Alooma's, but it was rapidly caving in. Sade's individualism was rejecting contributing and pushing out the Collective.

The Collective began to shrink, starting to retreat from their mind.

No . . . No!

If it shrank entirely, their pod could not become Gatherers. Naidon couldn't allow that.

He shut off every other connection, sensation, memory, even to Alooma—the disconnection from her splitting his body, and Naidon cried out in pain—instead, he focused solely on Sade. He recalled their first meeting. The spark between them. The look of need and hungry desire that flashed in Sade's eyes. He willed Sade to feel his presence until the two of them were alone in a dark void, pressing their palms together.

Sade had screwed his eyes shut, trembling. "No," he whispered. "Make them stop . . ."

"Shh." Naidon moved close enough so that he could rest their foreheads together. "Sade? Look at me." Sade shook his head. "It's okay. Whatever happened, happened. Don't be afraid of it. Let us help you."

Sade shook his head. "Negativity is not allowed in the Collective. I'll hurt our world. I can't . . . I can't join with you. I can't. I have to be alone."

For the briefest of moments, Naidon's awareness returned to what was happening in their shared mind—to Alooma and the shrinking Collective sphere. The bond between him and Alooma had also concaved. The Collective was collapsing in on itself. Alooma had screwed her eyes shut. More of her memories surfaced, hard, as if she were desperately trying to hold their pod together all by herself. Naidon couldn't stay focused exclusively on Sade for much longer. Not if he wanted their pod to succeed.

Closing his eyes and again shutting out everything but him and Sade, Naidon cupped Sade's face and made him look up.

"Listen to me, feel me. This is us. This is your future. Our future." He brought him in for a kiss that soon turned heated. Sade melted against him and opened his heart to Naidon—that was the only way Naidon could describe it. Sade willed Naidon to join with him. Naidon tried to help Sade remember his meeraid parental's memories, but anything Sade obtained just slipped through his mind so quickly it might as well have not existed.

This wasn't going to work. At this rate, they weren't going to be able to contribute enough to the Collective.

Just then, Alooma's presence sought them out so that now she stood with Sade and Naidon in the black void. She wrapped her arms around them both. That gave Naidon extra strength. Sade desperately tried to cling on to Naidon, fearful and panicking.

Naidon dug deep and searched for everything he could recall of his own meeraid parental's memories. Their pod had existed for far longer than seven parental joinings. The strength he felt told him as much. And although he had vastly stronger memories from his udon parental, he could tap into his meeraid parental's memories if he focused enough. It wouldn't be as strong as if Sade used his own memories, but it would have to do.

He focused only on Sade again. And even though Alooma was present—he desperately used her strength to hold him together—Naidon closed off his mind enough to her, taking Sade into an even deeper void where only they existed.

He used Sade and his connection and started to feed his meeraid parental's memories into Sade. He hoped that the spark between them proved enough of a link for Sade to act as a channel.

A flash of meeraid memory came across their shared mind. Then another one. And another.

Naidon continued to feed Sade his meeraid's parental memories until the bond between him and Sade was strong enough for Sade to reach inside of Naidon and then pull them out on his own.

Naidon's focus returned to the first black void where Alooma had also joined them—one step below their shared mind where they were feeding the Collective. A symbiotic relationship developed between the three of them. Alooma helped ground Naidon as he drew out his meeraid parental's memories. And since Naidon used Sade as a channel, the sensations that Alooma felt were not detected as coming from her former meeraid.

Then Naidon returned to their pod's shared mind. The beam that connected his palm to Alooma's glowed powerfully. It was long enough not to be pressing up against the Collective, but wasn't as straight as it had been when they'd first started.

The line connecting him to Sade also glowed brightly. As with Alooma, it wasn't straight. In fact, it was bowed noticeably, but it still helped to form a triangle, even if a curvy one. Alooma and Sade's beam was still the weakest and most deformed, but it was enough that their bond remained a triangle and not a circle.

Despite their pod's connection being weaker, it seemed to pacify the Collective. Inside the triangle, the sphere began growing again.

Images and flashes of memories that all three of them experienced dashed around the entirety of their joined mind as the Collective absorbed them.

Naidon returned to recalling his udon parental's memories, displaying everything inside of him in their shared mind. His memories were splashed by Alooma's. Seeing hers filled him with nostalgia and peace—as if he'd been present at every one of these events. He smiled at her, and her expression mirrored his own.

Sade's meeraid memories, which were still coming from Naidon, lit up the shared mind, filling in any gaps and overlapping other memories. The familiarity Naidon felt at them was strong, and he remembered what it was like to have loved his meeraid over the many cycles too numerous to count.

Something felt off about these memories. They came from Naidon's parentals, not Sade's, but maybe since Sade was the one channeling them, Sade's presence was coloring them somehow.

Alooma smiled softly at both him and Sade. Perhaps that was another reason why Alooma didn't discover his ploy. That strangeness that Sade's presence brought to the memories seemed to be enough for her to think these were Sade's actual memories.

Sade's expression held longing—for acceptance, for peace, for love. Naidon wouldn't deny him. He opened his heart, letting all his feelings for his pod burst forth, and it was like the three of them joined together again, even in their shared mind.

He'd been correct about Sade's connection to him. And in turn, Alooma had formed a connection to Sade, as he did to her. It was on this mutual connection between them that Naidon focused, as did Alooma, and the moment Sade did as well, the Collective grew with every sensation. Naidon could only imagine how much more intense this experience would be having come from another planet where they'd spent a substantial time on behaving and learning from the local life forms.

The Collective expanded and expanded until it finally engulfed them. For a single moment, Naidon felt like he both existed and didn't exist at all, like he was completely one with every maidoa that ever lived, past or present. Then the moment passed.

As the Collective retreated from their shared mind, Naidon returned to the world outside the sphere. He and his podmates were still joined.

Finally, he felt his body pulling away as they regained their individuality. When he opened his eyes, he found Alooma and Sade next to him. All three of them were palm to palm as they had been when they started.

They looked around as if noticing each other with new eyes, like they remembered who they were before, but also that they were separate. Themselves. Not simply reincarnations of their parentals. Sure, they had their parentals' memories, but they weren't their parentals. They were Sade, Alooma, and Naidon.

Alooma smiled widely, and she let out a laugh. Before they joined with the Collective, they didn't even know what laughter was, much less how to do it, but it seemed Alooma had already made it her own.

"We did it!" She threw her arms around them both and pulled them close. "I can't believe it! We actually did it!"

Pulling back, she kissed Sade deeply. "I knew you were one of us. I just knew it somewhere in my heart. And now I'm correct. Not only were your family Gatherers, but we meshed so well, it was like we were all of the same pod."

Naidon's chest ached, and he sucked in a breath, suddenly feeling afraid, guilty. Somehow Alooma hadn't realized that the meeraid memories she'd seen were her own parental's.

But how?

It was because of her connection to Sade. It existed primarily through Naidon, as Sade's connection to Alooma also was through him.

Sade relaxed into her hold, a soft smile playing on his lips. "Yeah. We did."

Naidon watched his two lovers with a gentle expression. Inside, though, his conscience tugged at his heart. He'd cheated. The only reason they'd been able to succeed was that Naidon had used the meeraid from his parental memory and not Sade's. Would Alooma figure this out? If she did, would she feel betrayed?

What would happen to them if they went out into the universe as Gatherers with a non-unified pod?

What had he gotten himself into? They couldn't redo the procedure until the next cycle, and by then, they would have gone on many harvests.

If other maidoas found out about their cheating, that would really shame his pod and his parentals as well.

No, Naidon was in too deep to back out now. He had to trust his instincts. Maybe his pod wasn't as strong as it would've been if they'd joined with their biological meeraid podmate, but the connection between him and Sade was real enough that Naidon had been able to use Sade as a channel. If they really were destined to fail, Sade's mind would've rejected it upon impact, but he didn't.

Alooma and Sade's relationship also didn't completely collapse, despite all that happened. Yes, it existed through him, but they were building one of their own, however slowly. After a few cycles, his pod would become strong in its own way. Question was, would their connection be enough to survive numerous cycles like their parentals had?

Sade looked over to him, and his smile faded. He knew what Naidon had done.

Naidon hugged him, trying to convey his feelings. "This is right," he whispered into Sade's ear.

Sade simply nodded and leaned into him.

Alooma hugged Sade from behind, resting her head on his back, her arms going around him until she caught hold of Naidon. "I can't wait to tell our parentals!"

Naidon nodded and allowed himself to feel the joy of their victory. This was right. He knew it, and Sade believed him. As for Alooma . . . he couldn't tell her the truth. He wouldn't outright lie to her, but if she never asked, then she'd never find out. Back in the ocean, he'd promised he wouldn't lie to her again. Omission was still a lie, although a soft one, but he would keep his other promise to her. He'd simply spend the rest of their lives making it up to her like he said on the Birthing Wall before they chased after Sade.

After their tiresome ordeal with the Collective, they decided to retreat to their own home—a bubble made especially for them. Then in the morning, they would share the good news.

About the Author

Melissa writes character-driven fiction, and any genre is fair game. When she's not writing, she enjoys reading, anime, manga, and gaming. Living by the motto of trying all things twice, Melissa has jumped out of a perfectly good plane, swum with manatees, dived headfirst into Alice's rabbit hole, and seduced classy ladies in 6-inch heels. A free-spirited bohemian, she currently lives in artsy St. Petersburg, Florida, with her soulmate and their two adorably needy cats.

www.ingramcontent.com/pod-product-compliance
Lightning Source LLC
La Vergne TN
LVHW020654100826
845148LV00012B/2492

* 9 7 8 1 4 8 7 4 3 2 3 9 3 *